C000213497

1

The day after in London

© *Nathanaël AMAH , 2020   NATHAM Collection*

Cover : Larisa KAZAKOVA

3

The day after in London

From the same author :

(E-books & paper version)

- Somewhere in Vladivostok
- Harcèlement   *(éd. BOD)*
- Harassment   *(éd. BOD)*
- Acoso   *(éd. BOD)*
- Neith (La mystérieuse Nubienne)   *(éd. BOD)*
- The Nubian (The mysterious Neith)   *(éd. BOD)*
- Les macarons   *(éd. BOD)*
- La veuve PLYNN   *(éd. BOD)*
- Instants ultimes   *(éd. BOD)*
- Que dire de plus ?   *(éd. BOD)*
- Cousine !   *(éd. BOD)*
- *T*u n'es pas la femme de l'homme
                    que je suis   *(éd BOD)*
- Londres : le jour d'après   *(éd BOD)*

(www.bod.fr)

The day after in London

The day after in London

THE DAY AFTER IN LONDON

Novel

The day after in London

1

In the British Airways Airbus that's taking her from Berlin to London, Maïa is in an indescribable state of distress.

Occasionally, she opens her bag, pulls out a sky blue silk scarf, brings it closer to her face and inhales at length the perfume it smells.

Then she carefully puts it in the bottom of her handbag and starts thinking about what she has lived in this German town that she just left half an hour ago.

The historical impact of the destruction of the Berlin wall has crossed German borders. All over the world, Berlin has become the symbol of this newfound freedom, the place where all "free" men and women feel a little more this atmosphere of total freedom, and consider themselves as citizens of this city that they appropriate gladly.

« *All free men, wherever they live, are citizens of this city of West Berlin, and for this reason, as a free man, I say : Ich bin ein Berliner* »,

had declared J. F. K in his famous speech in June 1963.

Delivered in its time and in another context, this speech illustrates the state of mind that everyone today can measure and appreciate its importance.

This fundamental freedom cannot be alienated for reasons of pure political ideology.

And so, at a time when Maïa was planning to organize this meeting which should allow her to live in real life this love experience that she had dreamed of, and to hatch this love that she patiently and secretly sheltered in her heart, Berlin had imposed itself on her.

She cannot explain this choice. Geopolitics was the least of her worries.

At the time of her choice, she felt inhabited by this strange love that she had not seen born but which she fiercely protected, like an embryo within her body. She felt that she had an obligation that she would have to meet at all costs. A goal to be achieved in her life as an adult woman, held in the crotaming between her life as a married woman, and that feeling of belonging to another man.

For her, there is no contraindication to be in such a position.

For, she is no longer satisfied with this conventional life established by the society of men. The one that imposes fidelity, restraint, decorum. On the other hand, she cannot ignore her deep desire to experience something new through the audacity that enabled the organization of this meeting.

She compares this situation to that of a child to whom the parents would have imposed a religion at birth, and once reaching the age of reason, that child, while assiduously praticing the parents's religion, on behalf of his/her sacrosanct freedom, would live with his/her own religious convictions. In other words, as far as she's concerned, living a passion outside marriage, can't taier the reputation of her status as a model wife, as long as it remains platonic.

2

Maïa is an independent person and a free spirit.

Her whole life has been marked by decision-making of which logic follows only her own logic.

She loves nature, the great outdoors, endless walks in the mountains.
Her adventurous spirit has inspired her many times to travel the world in search of new

landscapes, new encounters and new vibrations.
She travelled half the world and brought back lasting memories.

Her favorite film is "The River of No Return" by OTTO PREMINGER.

She has seen this film countless times with the same wonder.

For her, this film illustrates her vision of love and the whole process that leads to the outbreak of love.

She thinks of Marilyn MONROE and Robert MITCHUM, both involved in this process that leads to the outbreak of the most unlikely love.

When you sail the river of love, she says, the return is impossible.
This is so true for her that, any resistance is futile once the process of going to the other or accepting the other is engaged.
For, this process that inoculates this subtle or mysterious substance that no chemist can

reproduce in his laboratory, insinuates itself quietly, day after day in the brain the most devious, and finally and against all odds disables the discernment in most cases. Thus, reason gives way to unreason.

Time and time again, since her arrival, Maia has wondered about the real reasons for her presence in Berlin.

This new journey does not arouse the same emotions that she is used to experiencing with each of her travels around the world. She feels it very strongly, but can't explain it.

Indeed, while keeping herself active thanks to her wanderings in the city, she does not allow herself to be invaded by an overflowing enthusiasm. It's almost as if she's waiting for an event more important than her presence in this city of Berlin where her curiosity and critical thinking are solicited on every street corner.

She simply stores images, smells, noises for further analysis. At least, she hopes so.

3

At the end of this early autumn morning, a light rain fell on the city. It is a rain that is not spectacular, but one that wets terribly as long as we're without an umbrella .

Maïa takes advantage of this change of the weather to take a break from her day's program. She takes shelter in this typical German brewery in Uhlandstrasse, and decides to order a traditional pork shank

The day after in London

accompanied by sauerkraut and potato, a dish very caloric and which is appreciated with a good German beer as it's necessary to do it, according to the tradition.

During this lunch break, she was able to observe with astonishment and aversion, the clientele well fleshed out of this brewery, a heavy consumer of deli meats and beer, she who pays very attention to her diet and her shape. She wonders how to reconcile her desire to discover this very caloric German gastronomy with the rigor that she has always imposed to control her weight by the gram.

Fortunately for her, her stay in Berlin lasts only a week. So there is no risk of freaking out her scale at her return to London, at the moment she will weigh herself, as she used to do it every weekend.

She won't have to clog her ears when she'll get on her talking electronic scale.

She barely touched her meal to the astonishment of the waiter who worries and questions her with his eyes. She makes him understand that she just wanted to know the taste of this typical dish of the country. So, no proven sprain to her draconian diet.

Back into her hotel room, Maïa decided to take a nap. What is contrary to her habits. She is one of those people who think that taking a nap is a colossal waste of time. She thinks that a day is not enough to do everything or see everything. But, at this very moment when all her mind is turned towards the arrival of the one for whom she has braved so many certainties, so many forbidden to see herself in such a situation in Berlin, this nap can only be beneficial for her balance during the evening, provided that she manages to close her eyes and make the void in her mind.

She undressed, spent a brief time in the bathroom, then returned, wearing a white T-shirt (size XXL) on which it is inscribed "JUST DO IT".

She crept into her bed, and against all odds sank into a deep sleep.

Two hours later, she awoke startled.

She's sweating.

She emerges from a nightmare.

« ... *You're trying to make me angry, but you've exhausted all the rage I have in me... All I have left is disappointment....* »

The last sentence she remembers when she opens her eyes, a little lost in that big bed in which she has been sleeping for two days.

Against who was she fighting over in her nightmare?

Here she is, sitting in bed, leaning against the wall, immersed in her thoughts. She's thinking. She doesn't understand.

4

She eventually wakes up completely.
Her sleeping face is now lighting up.
She's thirsty.
She picks up the handset, calls the room
service and orders a cup of bergamot tea.

A moment later, the room service brought the
bergamot tea, accompanied by a plate of
Buchty Brioche, a brioche made with fresh
cream, unlike the French brioche more rich in

butter, what is much better for her hunt for extra pounds.

She sate down and enjoyed her tea-time with appetite, having eaten almost nothing during her lunch break in the brewery.

After this moment of pure happiness, she returned to reality.

The famous phrase still resonates in her head. She seemed angry. She tries to remember her nightmare which left her with a curious impression, but to no avail.

Maïa is not the kind of person to be angry for a yes or a no. Moreover, she rarely has dreams, let alone nightmares. This is what she claims in front of her friends. But if we stick to the claims of the experts on the dream domain, everyone has dreams. We still have to be able to remember that. But that is not the point. For now, despite this delicious Buchty Brioche that she has just tasted, there remains in her an impression of bitterness. Isn't it said that, little bitterness corrupts a lot of sweetness? What's behind the bitterness?

Where can it come from? However, everything should help to put her in a good mood. This unbearable expectation, this prospect of an embrace (even friendly) in the arms of the very one who managed to turn her life upside down to the point of making her unreasonable, everything should allow her to surf the waves of this overexcitement that she can no longer contain. But against all odds, her presence in Berlin (placed under the sign of an expectation that should make her hover and make her touch the peaks of happiness), gradually makes her uncomfortable. Her presence in Berlin seems to cause in her a real earthquake of which consequences she cannot measure.

What are the options available to her?

Either she packs her suitcase and takes the first flight back to her home in London as soon as possible, or she remains true to her commitment to meet this man who arrives by the 6pm flight. In this case, she should manage to resynchronize herself with her state of mind for more consistency in her attitude when he will take her in his arms.

On reflection, this nightmare she has just experienced during her nap, is it not the result of an internal conflict that does not say its name? What seemed to be an argument with a person she does not remember, could it not simply be the projection of the profound disagreement between her conscience and her unreason? Between her desire to express in the open, this fundamental freedom that she claims forcefully, and her status as a married woman subject to rules that contradict the very principles of this freedom that are imposed to each member of the couple, and more specifically to the woman whose value (in men's society) is measured by her ability to silence her feelings and behave in an exemplary manner?

If we try to extrapolate, and without wishing to make a particular case a school case, would the very foundation of the couple be called into question?

No, apparently not.

This is not a questioning induced by this or

22   The day after in London
© *Nathanaël AMAH , 2020   NATHAM Collection*

that behaviour within the couple. Indeed, an absence, a recreation, a trip, a getaway (as many denominations more or less poetic as can be imagined depending on the circumstances) are events that could shock the well-meaning souls, installed and evolving in an asceptized, codified and immutable Judeo-Christian society.

In short, a well-oiled and unavoidable routine. But isn't the couple the privileged place of all the upheavals, of all the changes, of all the surprises, of all the excesses, even of all the dangers?

Yes : the upheavals in all our certainties, the changes in our habits, the overconfidence in the other, the danger of our disillusionments, the surprising state of situation at the time of the assessment, all this contributes to considering the couple as the space of all mutations.

Maïa's questioning of her presence in Berlin takes her back a few years, the time when she could claim to be the woman of the dreams of someone for whom she's important more than anything.

It was the blessed time when the mere fact of going to the grocery store was the subject of proper prior communication : "*Honey, I'm going to do some shopping*.".

And gradually, over the years, from this rich communication, indispensable to the cohesion of her couple, she has moved on to this stage of minimalist communication, that of terse phrases such as : "*I'm going out.*".

Therefore, it is not surprising that she left, with a light heart to the unknown, without worrying about the situation before and after her trip to Berlin.

5

Maïa takes a look at her watch.

5 pm.

« *Oh my God* ».

She leaps out of bed and rushes into the bathroom.

A quick shower. A light make-up, then, heading to the airport.

Nestled in the back seat of the taxi that takes her to the airport, Maia starts her mobile and feverishly consults her e-mail.

Does she secretly hope to receive a message of renunciation from that person for whom her life is changing? Her inner conflict continues to torn her between this desire to fulfill this wish which she considers to be the commitment of her life, (a moment of her life that she cannot miss for all the gold of the world) and her desire to flee far away in order to avoid this moment that she is about to live and which would sign the end of all her certainties.

Certainties or easements ?

What about the reality of her married life?

Did free-will have a place in her everyday life, and more so, at the time of her decision to make this encounter to which she was so attached?

The day after in London

What can be the price to pay after the realization of her dream that became a real obsession?

The enthusiasm generated by the prospect of this meeting had created in her all the conditions to achieve this certainty that there is another life outside the couple.

But the state of total dependence on this "ghost love" and the idea she has of it, a state of dependence in which she recognizes herself, is not so different from the state of dependence she was accustomed to within her couple. Seen from the outside, she cannot escape the state of total conscious or unconscious dependence that she is about to experience, since this state induces the same degree of submission that she grants to her husband.

Basically, when you think about it, what's going to change for her?

Is it worth it?

By guessing, what will change for her by going to the end of her wish and her desire to live this love whose hatching is approaching, is that she will emerge from this mental or physical confinement induces by this marital experience.

By doing so, Maïa will probably be able to convince herself that she is not the woman of a single life. This would not systematically make her an umpteenth woman who would be separated or divorced, the motivations in this field being impressive. No, what could differentiate her from the other wives who would dare this misbehaviour is to make a deviation from an established situation, apparently healthy, which would endanger her certainties when everything seems to be going well. The killing of a couple which is not in agony, (always seen from the outside).

6

5:45 p.m. Berlin Schönefeld Airport.

The taxi has just come to a stop in front of the gate of the arrivals area.

The driver (Polish origin), remained silent during the way, stops the meter and announces the amount of the race.

Thirty-five euros.

The day after in London

Maïa rummages through her bag and eventually finds her wallet. She pulls out a fifty-euro bill. The driver returns her the change. She gets out of the taxi and rushes into the airport.

On the flight bulletin board, the aircraft has half an hour late.

Half an hour's respite or an extra chance to weigh up the pros and cons of her act ?

Meanwhile, she wanders through the arrivals area, nervously swinging her handbag back and forth.

Then, the voice of the hostess announcing the arrival of the flight, has made her tension raise a notch.

Maïa has trouble breathing. A slight dizziness forces her to stop her wandering in this area of arrivals that had filled with people without her noticing. She's frozen.

But, feminine coquetry obliges, she opens her handbag, feverishly searches for her pocket

The day after in London
© *Nathanaël AMAH , 2020   NATHAM Collection*

mirror. She eventually finds it and looks at herself in the mirror. It may be too late to rectify her makeup, but she's fine. The eyes are a little red, but her mascara has not flowed. It's a chance. She's presentable.

This endless time between the arrival of the flight and the actual exit of the passengers (because of the formalities), is not made to make things right.

Maïa wants to put an end to this wait.

Mechanically, she's heading for the exit. A stone's throw from the door, she makes a stop, then turns around.

The first passengers finally enter the arrivals area, tired and a little disoriented by the flight, but very happy to have arrived.

First hugs behind trolleys filled with luggage.

First emotions of lovers who meet again.

Maïa observes all this commotion without moving. She's paralyzed of fear.

The area is gradually emptying.

Among the few passengers still present, Maïa notices this silhouette that seems familiar to her, at least, that reminds her of someone seen a million times on Skype.

Her legs don't carry her anymore.

The silhouette moves towards her with an assured step. Maïa remains motionless. The silhouette is now a meter away from her. Then with a low voice: "**Hello Maïa !**".

7

Is she having a daydream? This voice that she knows well by interposed computer, now resonates in her ears in real life. How is that possible, she thinks.

Then the silhouette leans towards her, and gives her a single kiss on her left cheek.
She lets herself be touched. She doesn't know how to react. Should she take him by the neck, put her head on his chest, take his hands, or give him a kiss in return, as if she

wants to exorcise this state of intense feverishness in which she finds herself? She suddenly forgot everything she had promised to do at that very moment when she would see this man for the first time in person.

This is the first time in her life as a married woman that she has been approached so closely by a man who is not one of her relatives.

Curious feeling indeed.

She's invaded by a mixture of feelings and sensations she did not know. It vaguely reminds her of how she felt the first time she offered her nudity to her husband. Violence done by her, on herself. A form of capitulation in the face of the inevitable. An erasure of her person. A renunciation of her moral and physical integrity. A plunge into the unknown. At the time, she had wondered if it would hurt her this first time with her husband, today, for that first kiss on her left cheek, the pain, (even if she felt it as a form of betrayal), is not the same. This pain generated by the breaking of an oath made to a person deemed "dear" to her heart, cannot leave visible traces on her person. Only her heart recorded this intense, unforgettable emotion.

What about her consciousness?

Does the voice of her soul make weight against the voice of her body?

From the confrontation of her consciousness opposed to her passion, which will emerge victorious? Is she able to referee this match, the consequences of which she is not unaware of, since the rules are wrong since the beginning, rules of which she wrote every detail before flying to Berlin?

Faced with this lack of reaction, the man, taken by doubt, takes a step back and questions her :

– « *You're Maïa, aren't you?* »

A few seconds later, then :

– « *Of course, of course! ... I'm Maïa. ... Nice to meet you.* »

Maïa finally came out of her torpor, dares to say something.

The man's face suddenly lights up.

On track, Maïa adds :

- « *Good flight?* »

- « *Yes excellent flight. It went well. How about you? Is everything okay? ... I can see you're a little tense. Is there a problem? ... Do you want me to take the flight home right now?* »

said the man with a clenched smile on his lips.

Maïa's coldness contrasts singularly with her warm image on Skype. It's day and night. He can't believe this mixed welcome reserved for him. He had another idea of this meeting, the idea of which gradually matured in his mind. From then on, he asks to himself a thousand and one questions. There is a real questioning about Maïa's presence in this place, (she who is at the origin and initiator of this meeting), and the idea of a hypothetical renunciation that would have sprouted in her mind and that she could not (or cannot) express in a way frontal not to shock him, he who is so kind, he who agreed to cross all this way to see her.

   –   « ***What do we do now?*** »

he asks.

Maïa remains silent, but continues to stare at him. He doesn't understand anything.

   –   « ***If that's the way it is, I go to my hotel. When you'll decide to talk to me, you'll tell me. You know where to find me. Good bye Maïa !*** »

Immediately said, immediately done.

He rushed into a taxi that moved away, leaving Maïa alone in front of the taxi station.

The electroshock produced in her by the hasty departure of this disoriented and visibly disappointed man, brutally brings her back to reality.

She feels lost. She's cold. She's shaking. She doesn't understand what just happened. This is not what she had imagined. What happened ? she wonders. She really doesn't understand. How can she correct the situation? What image will he keep of her? What can she do to erase the shame she has covered herself with?

8

The first experience in any situation, however exceptional, can lead to a disaster possibly announced.

A first blow in a matrimonial relationship cannot leave unscathed the one by whom the "scandal" happens (according to the well-thinking Judeo-Christian society).

The marital bond, however invisible, cannot

break at the first gale, however violent it may be.

Maïa seems to experience it terribly, this one of the invisible presence of the very one who is at the other end of this invisible bond. This invisible presence that seems to thwart any attempt to erase it from the scene at a T-moment.

« *The excuse of infidelity is that there is nothing as pleasant as the beginnings of love.* », wrote Édouard HERRIOT in his notes, thoughts and maxims in 1961.

But that's not how Maïa feels, chilled, alone, standing in front of the Berlin taxi station, at this very moment. She would like the earth to open under her feet and be swallowed up whole, from head to toe, without any of her hair remaining on the surface of the earth.

The same sneaky rain as in the late morning, begins to fall. Maïa decides to leave the airport. She gets into a taxi, and gets dropped off at her hotel.

In the taxi that took her back to the hotel, she couldn't help to sob and to burst into tears.

The taxi driver, a native German, tried to solicit her attention in the rearview mirror, driving his taxi only with one eye. He guessed Something happened at the airport. He was sorry he couldn't help her.

And when he cashed the race, he dared telling her in English without any accent:

"*I'm so sorry!*".

Maïa replied with a smile before leaving the taxi.

A hot shower and, in bed. Tomorrow it will be daylight.

In the middle of the night, she woke up with fright : the same nightmare. This time, the dispute was a little more violent. But, as in the early afternoon, no precise memory of her interlocutor. Just the memory of a grave and vehement voice, a strange disapproving vocal expression that put her in a state of fear, making her heart beating very hard when she woke up.

This obvious antagonism, which is expressed repeatedly, makes her uncomfortable vis-a-vis her plan to live a love story outside of her marital relationship.

Who can prevent her from carrying out this project, if not herself ?

This obvious sign of a serious internal conflict that has paralyzed her since the end of the rainy morning and which worsened with the arrival of the 6 pm flight, does not seem to predispose her to more audacity in the fight against the prohibitions enacted by society. Judeo-Christian to her own values as a woman free of influence but who does not want (or does not seem) to give herself the right to accede to her unspeakable desires.

For now, after several attempts, she manages to get back to sleep.

9

After a dashed night, Maia emerged from her sleep very late, awakened by the housekeeper.

She's having a hard time concentrating. She's got a terrible headache . She's got a hangover without drinking a drop of alcohol. A big desire to vomit. She shows a slight tremor.

She picks up the handset and calls the front desk.

No calls for her. No message for her.

She looks at her watch. It's 10:30 am. The morning is almost over. Still no solution to repair the disaster of the previous day. What can she do about this man who, in his last sentence before getting into his taxi: « *... **You know where to find me.*** », de facto has assigned her the responsibility of this fiasco. Clearly, it is up to her to decide whether or not they will see each other again. She is well aware of this: even if she adopts an apparent relaxation, the fire burns within her. She doesn't know how to put out it off. Does she know so little about herself? Did she presume her willingness to break this prohibition that seems to torment her so much? What did she come to Berlin to do?

For the time being, the four walls of her room provide her with pseudo security in the face of this decision that she should make but which is slow to come.

After a long moment, lounging in her bathtub, her decision is made.

Maia tries to appear acceptable. No war paint on the face, no peace pipe in the hand. Just her, Maia in all her splendour, eager to assume her responsibilities.

She orders a cab.

A moment later, the reception announced the arrival of the taxi.
A last check in front of the bathroom mirror, the raincoat over the shoulder and then, Maia quietly took the lift without hurrying.
Last stop. The elevator's door opens and frees its occupants. In the lobby of the reception, many people: entrances and departures follow one another at the counter.

She crossed the crowd and finds herself outside, determined to move forward.Yes, but to what, to whom? She did not forget her fiasco the day before at the airport.
She settled in the back of the taxi, which started immediately.

During the journey, she feels a fever rising again in her. This fear that had destroyed her the day before, was invading her again. But this time, she doesn't let it happen. She straightens her back, opens her purse, takes out her mobile and calls her husband in London.

Two ringtones, then Henry's voice.

- "*Hello darling.*" she says.

A long silence that seemed to her an eternity and then, at the other end of the line :

- "*Good morning.*"

A frosty, sharp voice that freezes her blood.

Maïa doesn't know what to say. She doesn't even know why she made this crazy decision to call her husband.

She is on her way to what she considered an essential step in her life as a woman. A step that, for her, should reinforce her idea that she does not belong to anyone.

- "*I just want to give you my news and to know how you're doing. ... Are you okay?* "

- *"**Where are you?**"* asked the abandoned husband.

Spontaneously, without any discernment regarding the profound meaning of this question, Maïa dared this unexpected answer that everyone would disapprove of :

- *"**In a taxi.**"*

A long silence, then :

- *"**Where are you?**"* asked again Henry raising the tone.

- " ***In Berlin.*** " finally replied Maïa with a falsely detached voice.

- *"**And can you tell me what you're doing in Berlin?**"*

- *"**Nothing. ... I'm visiting.**"*

Henry is stunned. He's disgusted. He doesn't know what to say. He chooses to end the communication.

Maïa sighs, then puts her mobile at the bottom of her purse and waits patiently for the end of the journey.

10

In London, clouds pile up on Henry's head. His sky darkens, the storm is not far away. The persistent state of mind which is his own, generated by both surprise and fear as a result of this phone call, definitively turns his day into a bad day.

Indeed, after ending the hallucinating communication with Maïa, Henry rereads for the umpteenth time the terse message (scribbled hastily on a sheet torn from the old diary) found on the kitchen table on the day of his wife's departure.

– *"Honey, I'm leaving for a few days.* "

A terse message that does not specify the destination or the duration of the stay. None of that. Not even the manifestation of a semblance of affection of the style: "*I kiss you*," or the gleam of hope to see her again one day: "*see you soon.*" Just the minimum service to signify what seems to be "a mark of respect", unearthed from the depths of her being, with regard to the one she still considers her husband. In any case, the message left on the kitchen table seems to attest to this.

He usually didn't pay much attention for his wife's escapades.Until then, their relationship had not created any tension within their couple : one day she leaves, the next day, she comes back. Life continued smoothly. Both were satisfied with this pseudo-arrangement that allowed them to continue their life without asking metaphysical questions about how they functioned.

Everyone has a good reason to do it that way. And that's the main thing.

Yet he has experienced particular moments, even difficult ones with her, moments related to the events of the ordinary life of the couple, and which have not so far awakened in him this strange impression that the absence of his wife (who is abroad moreover), does not augur well.

It is not in her habit to leave England without talking about it profusely around her in all steps of the preparation of her trip.

It's one of her ways of communicating, and her enthusiasm is communicative. .

The local merchants always were the first to be informed of her travel projects, and always took advantage of her first travel impressions on her return. Thus, they could visit countries

51   The day after in London

© *Nathanaël AMAH , 2020   NATHAM Collection*

(at little cost), receive impressions of travel, dream in front of pics of distant landscapes accumulated in the gallery of her mobile phone.

That was the Maïa that everyone knew at home and outside.
The one who had no secrets for anyone, at least, regarding her travel intentions.

Homebody and deeply "British", Henry travels very rarely. He has a holy abhorrence to sleep in a bed other than his own. He has habits to which he almost never deviates: his tea-time is sacred. The hour of his dinner is invariably the same since a long time. As for his diet, he consumes only organic products that he goes to buy on the farms (himself) at the wheel of his Land Rover.

His walk in St James's Park, has become a ritual with a well-targeted route.
St James's Park is his favourite place.

It was during one of his daily walks in this place that he had met Maïa, who had just landed in London, visiting the Westminster area.

He likes to tell this story to his friends who have heard it a hundred times, a story whose tasty details have faded over time.

*"**The carriage of the past does not lead us anywhere,**"* wrote Alekseï Maksimovich Pechkov (Maxime Gorki).

Rightly so, Henry begins to glimpse the limits of this couple he forms with Maïa, and the deadlock in which he seems to find himself at this very moment.

Indeed, Henry's life alongside Maïa, as rich as it is in appearance, as interesting as it is from the exchanges point of view, is no less based on a fragile balance.

Until that fateful phone call from Maïa, (seen from the outside), their life as a couple was in fact a juxtaposition of two diametrically opposed lives, based on a tacit agreement established the day after they met in St James's Park

In fact, that day, providence was maneuvering
.

She had just arrived to England to officially take up an au pair position in a wealthy English family. But actually, her mission was different and twofold: on the one hand, to get used to the young teenager she had to care for (the only girl who was coming out of a serious nervous breakdown with several suicide attempts to her credit) to allow her to have a social life at home, to put an end to her loneliness and avoid to her to fall back on herself. On the other hand, implement her therapeutic method to treat the case of this teenager outside the official presence of a health professional in white blouse.

The choice of Maïa was a no-brainer for this family insofar as she is a well-known graduate psychologist, author of a proven method of treatment in her home country.

Henry is a film music composer. He is married for the third time and has no children from his union with Maïa. He spends most of his time in his studio located in the basement of his house in a suburb of London. Music is his whole life. He has a real passion for this art, which some have described as minor art.

In summary, two professions covering the only two areas of activity in the world without any connection, professions carried out by both without any possibility of intellectual interconnection, generating different interests that fuel day after day this growing disinterest in the common life, manifested by her and which translates in it into a greater desire for independence.

Cupidon's work that day in St James's Park was extraordinary. Because to succeed in attracting the attention of these two people to the point of making them a couple, is a real feat, which is quite remarkable.

As much as one is taciturn, cultivating the art of silence when he is not isolated in his studio to compose, the other is more voluble, hungry for human warmth and noises to precisely fill this silence that she has more and more difficulties to bear.

11

« *For a woman, getting married is like jumping in the river in the middle of winter: something you don't do twice.* »

Maïa knows it only too well.

If it is true that Henry did not steal her innocence, and that her experience as a woman until then (among other things) comes down to one or two homosexual adventures without a future on campus, at the time of her studies in her country of origin, preferring to get away from it before it is too late, before she gets attached, having failed to determine her deep nature as to her sexual inclinations, the fact remains that her entry into the marital life with this man was a real surprise for her, if not a real shock.

The fact that she arrived in this relationship that led her to this union with Henry, is the consequence of what she understood in Henry's answer when she clearly said to him (eye to eye) on the day of his wedding demand :

   "Love me without respite. Then I'll be yours, full and whole. »

Would Henry have heard another version of this requirement to the point of answering :

   "Yes, I promise you."

He, who had vowed not to find himself again

in such a process that reminds him of the infernal round of the butterfly around the bright flame of a lit candle.

A true renunciation of a resolution made and held since a long time. A renunciation worthy of what he hoped by lowering his guard against all odds. What has happened since the encounter in St James's Park is far from a succession of moments of bewilderment. Some would say that his appetite and thirst for life are not dry and that he would have matured in his quest for happiness.

Okay, but did he, through his meeting with Maïa, find a way to achieve this sublimation of this new marriage that would make it beautiful and eternal?

Failing that, don't we say, "*Never two without three*"?

His two previous marital experiences left a bitter taste in his mouth, emptied his wallet and installed in his mind a real aversion to the institution of marriage.

Since then, this union is similar to a dwelling with the doors that remain opened constantly: nothing obliges to stay, nothing prevents from leaving.

His credo : remain free in a relative happiness.

Henry managed to set up this system that would make any being who would feel cramped in his marriage pale with jealousy. To be able to preserve the independence of one's happiness despite of the vicissitudes of life.

But can we talk about a successful marriage if the man and woman in the couple do not have the wisdom to remain in the same place? If their eyes are resolutely outward-looking or riveted on the light signals on the ground indicating the exit? If all escape opportunities are the subject of special attention? If the unspoken became the rule and not the exception?

Assuming that in this cage with open doors, the bird ends up noticing the reality of its

59

condition, once gone, will it want to come back to drink the fresh and sweet water at the bottom of its cup?

Nothing is less certain.

12

In Berlin, Maïa's taxi has just arrived at its destination in front of the Albrechtshof Hotel on Albrechtstrasse.

She pays the taxi fare and gets out of the taxi.

She takes her pocket mirror out of her purse, opens it, checks her makeup for a while and then closes it and puts it at the bottom of the bag. Her eyes are a little bit tired but it doesn't matter. Everything else is okay. She's acceptable.

She walks through the door of the hotel and walks towards the front desk with a determined step. She waits her turn, then politely asks the receptionist to announce her arrival.

The receptionist tries to call the room 342.

- *"Sorry, the room isn't responding."* says the receptionist.

- *"Ah! And, do you know when he'll be back?"*

- *" Not at all madam. Can I get a message for him?"* declares the receptionist, showing some impatience.

- *" Yes, please. Tell him Maïa came by to see him. He'll understand. Thank you. Goodbye, madam. "*

As soon as she finished taking leave of the receptionist, before she had time to turn her heels to regain the exit of the hotel than, a familiar and reassuring voice calls her behind her back :

–   " *Maïa !* "

She turned around and saw this man whom she had come to conquer, determined not to be disturbed by anything.

He's sweaty, but his face is smiling.

He had just been jogging. He is preparing for the next New York Marathon. Running has become his favorite pastime, almost his second nature. He's in perfect physical condition. He's all in muscle. Maïa seems to find it out through her wet t-shirt. She's impressed. She had never had this vision of him on SKYPE. Her disturbance at the airport the day before also did not allow her to realize what kind of athlete's body she had in front of her.

While wiping his face :
  –   " *Finally you came?* "
he said without any triumphalism.

  –   " *Yes I did, as you can see.* "
replies Maïa, a bit shy.

  –   " *Go and take a sit in the lounge.
      I'm going upstairs to take a
      shower. ... Order a cup of coffee. ...
      See you later.* "

Maïa watches him walk away towards the
elevators. She can see him from back. Again,
she is impressed, captivated by this body,
built like an athlete from ancient Greece,
without really wondering what it hides.

She feels lighter to have broken the ice, even
if nothing is yet certified on the acceptance of
this man who has become a real enigma to
her, so much he impresses her.

She cannot believe that she focuses this way
on the physical aspect of a man. She does not
remember (as far back as her memory can
allow her to remember) of being disturbed by

the aesthetic aspect of a man. It's not her style to play the fanatic girl in front of the poster of an inaccessible star.

That's not why she came. She does not want to be disturbed by what she sees as interference that could scramble her speech. She needs the clarity of her mind to face her Greek athlete.

She knows why she's here in this hotel. She knows the reasons for her capitulation by going to this interrupted rendezvous instead of being on a flight towards London.

Therefore, in such a context, she must keep herself away from any distraction. She must concentrate and use this moment of the shower to prepare to get down into the arena for her announced killing.

13

In the shower, he lets hot water flow over his body. He is not in a hurry to return back in the lounge. He's thinking of her. He's taking all his time.

In fact, he was chilled by the frosty (or even bizarre) welcome that Maïa gave to him at the airport upon his arrival. He is not far from thinking that it was a very bad idea to have made the trip from Valletta to Berlin.

But how could he resist to this invitation for which Maïa has deployed all her talent to present him the good side of this experience that she dared to describe more than once, as the experience of a lifetime.

If life is an experience in its own right and, as Oscar Wilde quite rightly put it, that *"Experience is the name that everyone gives to his mistakes"*, how could he understand and integrate this idea of wanting to live this slice of life in Berlin, in search of this experience that should be the experience to live at any cost? Does that have another name?

The answer to this central question is probably found in the last epistolary exchanges on Skype, exchanges in which Maïa had been able to extol the necessary disobedience of wisdom in favor of a fleeting happiness that would help (according to her) to live the experience of a lifetime.

In practical terms, how should this necessary disobedience manifest itself at his level?

On reflection, he sees only one possibility: this disobedience should be based on his willingness or acceptance to be complicit in this adventure with the ultimate goal of putting a face on a first name, to feel in real life the effects of virtual kisses exchanged all this time on Skype or perhaps, his contribution to the realization of an exacerbated fantasy , prompting Maïa (filled with extreme desires) to convince herself that she does not belong to anyone.

In short, accepting to be the perfect alibi, which by nature generates ultimately and undeniably suffering on behalf of feelings used to justify what may be reprehensible in the good old Judeo-Christian society.

But (he thinks), Maïa's excessive ego is such that it's not able to allow her to realize this lie with respect to herself. Lie based on a certainty similar to the sketch of a heart on the sand by the sea and which disappears at the first surge of a powerful wave on the beach.

The next moment, everything disappears causing the return to reality. The tumultuous retreat of the mighty wave, taking everything to the bottom of the sea. A destructive backlash that spares neither feeling nor dreams.

This fleeting happiness, described as the experience of a lifetime, cannot hide the existence of an emotional desert, created from scratch by her, in which she is entangled in this relationship with this man named Henry.

14

Back in the lounge, he saw Maïa asleep, her purse squeezed against her chest.

He hesitated for a moment and then tried to wake her very gently.

Nevertheless, Maïa wakes up a little bit lost, and a little ashamed to have fallen asleep.

He reassures her and invites her to go to take a walk a little before lunchtime.

She agreed and, there they are, walking side by side without saying a word to each other.

That lasted a while, and then he decided to break the silence :

- *"Are you okay? "*

- *"Yes I'm, and you, are you okay? "*

- *"Have you been able to visit the city? ... You arrived before me, are there any interesting things to see in Berlin? "*

- *"Yes I think so, but actualy, I haven't really visited the city. I barely saw my neighborhood and its surroundings. I was waiting for you, looking forward to discover things with you. "*

- *" Oh! Looking forward ? "*

- *" Yes sir! Very impatient. ... Do you have any doubts? "*

71   The day after in London

Their faces display a broad smile.

– *" There is reason to doubt. No? ... Put yourself in my shoes. "*

Maïa's face becomes serious. She knows it's time to burst the abscess. She can no longer hide. She had prepared for this moment but does not really know how to approach the subject to defuse the smoldering anger. Suddenly, she grabs his arm and prevents him from moving forward. She stands in front of him and stares straight in his eyes. He can almost read the fear in her agate-colored eyes.

– *"Please, tell me, are you still angry against me?"*

she said, without being able to hide the anguish that undermines her.

– *"Yes, I'm still angry against you, to be honest with you. ... How would you have reacted if you were in my shoes? "*

Maïa remains silent, and visibly seeks to get closer to him to press her head against his chest. But he remains at a good distance and does not seem to allow her this intimacy.

Maïa still holds her hand firmly around his arm. She has no intention of releasing him until she is absolved of her great sin of the day before. And this absolution will necessarily have to go through this kiss that she has been dreaming of for many weeks. She wants that kiss right there, right in the middle of the street, in front of a church in red bricks. No matter the people around them. It doesn't matter if after this kiss, he lets her down in this street. She would not mind.

   –   *"I'm sorry."*
she said.

   –   *" Sorry about what?   Sorry about who ? I just want you to explain to me why you treated me this way. ... I can't understand why you behaved in this way with me. ... What did I do to you? Do you think I've come all this way to be humiliated like you did it?*

You know Maïa, I believed your story as a little boy to whom his mom promised a bag of treats, would do it. I believed it so much, you know. Now I don't know what to think. "

Maïa breathes a big sigh. She doesn't know what to say. She'd like to tell him something, but what? She feels shabby. The building, which she has been patiently building for several weeks, is cracking.

15

In Valletta, Kenneth works in the financial sector.

He lives a tidy life. He's disciplined, rigorous. Aptitudes required by his profession.

He practices running, but does not miss any football matches, a very popular sport in Malta.
Oddly enough, he never set foot in Ta' Qali

The day after in London

Stadium.

He hates to find himself in places where the density of the population prevents him from having absolute control over his environment.

The uncontrolled overflow of the crowd is a real obsession for him.

He's been dragging this phobia since he was a young boy.

Indeed, at a funfair in the city, under pressure of the crowd, he finally let go of his mother's hand who held him firmly. So caught by the crowd, like a giant wave that carried him off, away from his mother, it took several hours for the police to find him and return him to his family. It was a traumatic experience for him and since then he always has avoided being in the crowd.

This led him, once being adult, to focus on individual sports, with the exception of the practice of marathon, a sport for which he had to do a lot of work on himself to manage to be in the compact peloton of marathon runners at the start of the marathon.

Kenneth is a pragmatic person.

He adapts to reality and acts accordingly, concretely, completely, sincerely.

At a time when, by the most curious of chances his virtual route crossed that of Maïa, he had no preconceived idea of what this form of relationship between a man and a woman who do not know each other or who have never seen each other in the flesh in real life.

A hell of a discovery for him.

He gradually became captivated by this game of seduction which obeys no logic and which is based on no truth on either side.

As a general rule, saying "I love you" in a foreign language does not have the same flavour as in one's original language with all that it implies in direct connection with one's own culture.

So, what about these thunderous statements with hidden faces, (sometimes bordering on hysteria and over-bidding) promising mountains and wonders through interposed social networks, however sincere they may be but which do not oblige anyone?

Isn't it true that sometimes lightning falls on dry grasses and sets them ablaze causing irreparable damage?

Through this virtual relationship, and on the basis of this supposed sincerity that he showed from day one, sincerity which was the trigger of his determination to pursue this relationship beyond his convictions and which led him to Berlin, he always wanted to know what the effects might be induced by this experience that Maïa described as the experience of a lifetime.

He does not define himself as an opportunist, namely, one who does never deny himself but who often rallies.

Maïa is close to him, within his lips' reach.

He feels flattered by this outburst of feelings towards him.

But the day after : what will this next day look like, when everything will be consumed, when the fog of feelings that prevents us from seeing reality in front of us, is dispelled ?

For the time being, what will he do face in this situation in which he feels uncomfortable, in contrast to the idyllic image suggested and described by Maïa during their epistolary exchanges as the experience of a lifetime?

16

Still clinging to his arm, Maïa finally manages to lay her head against his chest. She was not rejected. It's not a torrid melee, but it's a good start. She can hear his heart beating. She feels a little more reassured but she's desperately waiting for the kiss she's been dreaming of for so long and still doesn't come. She is ready to climb up to his lips while standing on tiptoe, provided that her wait does not last too long. At her young age, the practice of classical dance and the rigor attached to it, have etched in her memory how painful it can be to stay on tiptoe beyond a certain threshold.

She has no choice: he is immensely tall and his lips are inaccessible. She does not know what to do to make it easier for her by stooping down a little bit. So, she tries an old trick :

  – *"I'm cold..... Take me in your arms, please. Please. "*

No effect after this plea sewn with white thread.

  – *" Let's go to lunch if you don't mind. ... You can warm up and regain your strength. "*

Replied Kenneth, looking detached.

  – *" Good idea Kenneth. What do you propose ? "*

She said, sporting her most sincere air.

– " *My hotel restaurant is correct. I have the advantage of having dinner there yesterday. That was good. .. We can return there unless you have another idea to suggest to me?* "

– " *No, it's perfect! I'm following you. ... I am hungry.* "

Immediately, they turn back and redirect to Albrechtstrasse. The hotel is not far away. Just a few more steps.

As soon as they arrived, they entered into the hotel lobby and headed to the restaurant under Kenneth's leadership.

Suddenly, Maïa makes a stop :

– " *Can I use your toilet please?* "

– " *I think there are toilets not far from the restaurant in the lobby. Do you want me to take you there?* "

Maïa has a hard time hiding her terrible

disappointment at making another shot that didn't hit its target.

She knew about these toilets. She had used them while he was showering and she waiting for him in the lounge. But, it was a great opportunity to penetrate his living space, which for now seems to be an impregnable citadel.

– " *Yes, Please.* "

So she follows him like his shadow up to the bathroom door. He opens the door and lets her in. He closes the door behind her. He waits patiently in the hallway, taking advantage of the hotel's WIFI to check his email on his smartphone.

Inside, Maïa stops in front of a bathroom sink and pours cold water on her hands which have a slight tremor. She's on the verge of a nervous breakdown. She fulminates by condemning herself for having acting like an idiot the day before at the airport.

Her heart is filled with bitterness. She's got a stomach ache.

This ordeal, which she self-inflicted, has so far ended in a bitter failure.

What was supposed to be the celebration of the newfound freedom, and which would have allowed her to get a brillant triumph over all these years of doubts, deprivations, restraints, ordered by her status as a married woman, is at this very moment a set of disappointments from which she needs and must manage the consequences.

She feels the unpleasant taste of something unfinished while, continues to burn in her, this irrational and untenable desire to satiate this need to achieve the goal she had set herself by going to Berlin. Despite her misfortune, she is optimistic. She did not come to find a new husband to replace her old husband who remained in London. But what she came for is more than that. She came to look for herself with the secret hope of lightening the weight of the past that pushed her out of her home. No matter the pitfalls that mark this path that she has set out to travel in her quest for happiness.

She fully understands Kenneth's reaction to

keeping his distance from this woman who may seem unbalanced to him.

She would have done the same, if not more. Perhaps she would even have returned to London after setting him on fire as that should be.

At first glance, Kenneth's attitude may seem contemptuous. Some might think that he is looking for a good reason to build a "shelter" allowing him to fall back if necessary. Others will judge him as the prudent man who would like to keep all his lucidity in this situation that could very quickly turn to tragedy, Maïa being able to believe in the existence of a consented and shared love between two adults in good faith and who would ultimately feel rejected, flouted, betrayed. Or he could be that impostor waiting for the right moment to act, the same one who pretended to be a reassuring gentleman who entered the seduction game initiated by Maïa by Skype interposed and who would have seduced her to the point of pushing her to desert her home.

At this point in history, opinions may diverge, in the face of Kenneth's overt inertia, who, taking into account current mentalities, could have jumped on his prey without asking metaphysical questions. He would have taken what would be graciously offered to him. End of the discussion.

What if Kenneth had simply come without preconceived ideas, as a "good friend" to visit a city of which Maïa has extolled its charms to him with weighty arguments, to the point of making him wanting to make the trip to keep her company ?

What do you think?

Maïa remains hopeful of turning the situation in her favour.
Still three days to spend in Berlin and Kenneth has not made and announced the decision to anticipate his return to Valletta.

17

It was the lunch of all dangers.

Distrustful, scalded, Maïa was sitting between two chairs.

On the one hand, the comfortable one of the reasonable, patient woman.
On the other, the uncomfortable one (similar to incandescent embers) of the woman ready to get angry.

Maïa can't say the composition of her menu during this surreal lunch, nor the name of the main dish she tasted.

Yet she looked good, laughing heartyly at Kenneth's many jokes, who turned out to be a true charmer.

His funny and incredible anecdotes captivated his guest, as naturally as on Skype.

He is attentive, persuasive, even managing to get her to receive the "beaked", i.e. to make her delicately open her mouth to deposit pieces of food taken from his plate, using his fork.

The atmosphere was almost perfect because of this connivance which (apparently) was in no doubt, and which knew (as if by magic) to mask her excruciating loneliness.

She ate with appetite at the same time to fill her stomach and to honor the invitation of her host, but this appetite is far from satisfying her ambition to carry out her project to the end.

How can we understand and explain that a well-oiled, long-developed mechanic, which is just waiting to work perfectly, can suddenly turn into a mountain of worries?

Isn't this the perfect illustration of what is the apocalypse?

It all starts with a bright morning, everything is fine throughout the day, and at the end of the day, it's the end of the world. No one knows what happened except that : it's nothingness, all of a sudden.

From that time of happy days when their two virtual roads crossed with the firm hope of a encounter full of promise, tenderness, voluptuousness, until this lunch during which, the flame of the candle (which illuminated their journey and illuminated their mutual desires to live this famous experience of a lifetime), wavered without being subjected to a strong north wind , Maïa's state of mind has changed somewhat.
The control of her emotions is undermined by her unwellness in this situation over which she no longer has any control.

She is facing an "enemy" that is not one. She does not feel able to face this adversary who has not declared war on her.

She finds it difficult to understand that the transition from the virtual to the reality of real life, must necessarily involve the complete reset of this relationship on the basis and the consideration of the feelings felt and developed by two individuals, "alive", driven by the same desire to love each other.

18

On the way back to her hotel with Kenneth, who decided to return the politeness by taking her home, Maïa wonders what to do about this case which drives her crazy.

This madness, which she would like to avoid at all costs, which pushes her irretrievably towards renouncing her initial urges to live the experience of her life, prevents her from clearly reading the intentions of the one for whom she created this upheaval in her own life without measuring its consequences.

On the one hand, there is Henry, remained faithful to his alliance with her and who awaits her firmly on her return to London, on the other, Kenneth who seems to play with her good faith and commitment to this adventure of which every step was meticulously prepared during the weeks leading up to her arrival in Berlin.

On both sides, the consequences are inevitable, knowing that any decisive action has its inevitable consequences. She knows that.

Either she leaves Berlin fully inflated after having lived this experience to which she is very attached, and once in London, her married life will take another turn, or she leaves Kenneth in tears, disappointed to have fooled herself, convinced that the one who made her believe that another life is possible, was finally not the same person who made her dreaming in front of her computer.

What to do about this situation that made her realize that she was being held when she thought she was holding?

Towards who to turn to console herself ? Who can help her to make the right decision? This saving decision (long awaited) that she will not regret at the end and which will make her proud to have dared.

So, against all odds:

– *"Tell me Kenneth, do you regret coming to see me?"*

– *"No, of course, Maïa. It was a great idea having proposed me this trip. Why this question?"*

– *"If I understand well, you just came to visit Berlin?"*

– *"Not at all !"*

– *"You came a little for me too, didn't you?"*

- *"I don't understand your question."*

- *"I had hoped for something else by coming here."*

- *"Something else like what, Maïa?"*

- *"That you and I could finally meet after everything we've said on Skype."*

Kenneth smiles.

- *"Yes, I understand what you're getting at."*

- *"So what? What are we going to do? What do you propose me?"*

Faced with this flood of questions, Kenneth makes a stop and turns towards Maïa.

- *"Maïa, what do you expect from me?"*

- *"Do you really want to know?"*

-    *"Yes, Maïa. Tell me. Please. "*

After a moment of hesitation, she throws herself into the water.

-    *"I would like to share a night with you. Just one. Is that possible? "*

Kenneth smiles again to hide his embarrassment.

-    *"Is this important to you?"*

-    *"Yes, it's important! ... Not for you? "*

-    *"I didn't ask myself that question."*

-    *" Oh ? ... Ok ! "*

-    *"You seem angry."*

-    *"No, I'm not ! Just a little disappointed. I thought you cared a little bit about our love story, too. "*

-    *"Our love story? What do you mean?*

Can you explain it to me? "

—   *" No, let it go. Well, I'm going to get a cab back to my hotel. I am tired. Goodbye Kenneth. Good end of the day. "*

No sooner said than done. Maïa turns her back on him, beckons the first taxi that passes nearby, and takes leave of her host who remains frozen on the sidewalk in this street not far from his hotel.

He looks at the taxi driving away, a little stunned, surprised by Maïa's reaction who did not give him time to explain himself.

19

After a few hours wandering around the city, Kenneth finally returns to the hotel for a break before dinner. But when he arrived in his room, he saw the package he had prepared for Maïa. A gift he brought back from Valletta for his friend Maïa.

He immediately came out, took a taxi and went to Maïa's hotel to give her this gift that was close to his heart.

So, he handed the package over to the hotel reception, not wanting to see her again, assuming her state of mind after what had happened in the early afternoon. He just wanted her to know that he cares about her, not as she would have liked, but enough to have prepared and brought back this gift to her as his attachment to her, and to extend their meeting in Berlin when she'll return to London.

Then he went away with a light heart.

She will do as it'll please her with that, he says, with the secret hope that his gift will please her beyond her resentment.

He doesn't believe that Maïa is the woman of resentment.

From what he perceived of her during those long weeks of discussion with her on Skype, it was first and foremost her propensity to never be burdened with resentments of any kind, whatever the reason. It's too heavy to carry like she told him. The liberation of the soul, is according to her, the only and best way to heal after a psychological shock. Therefore, there was never any question for her to mourn an offence, if there is an offense.

Kenneth tries to reassure himself as much as he can, by assuming, by convincing himself that the incident is over.

But who can measure the consequences of an intense emotion felt by a woman whose heart has been broken? Who can presume the reactions of the woman in love who would feel humiliated and neglected?

Maïa had fallen madly in love with Kenneth to whom she had opened her heart, to whom she was ready to give her body as a token of this love that she maintained in secret. She had managed to captivate him to the point of making him make this journey to Berlin, when there was no obligation. Everything was on track. But.....

What didn't work?

Why did she feel like a person who is desperately trying to cling to the water around her to avoid drowning?

20

When he returned from his jog the next morning, the receptionist gestured Kenneth to give him an envelope. He thanks her and goes up to his room. He puts it on the bed and directly goes to shower.

He's taking all his time. Then he decides to open the envelope and read its contents.

First reflex : the signature at the end of the

message: Maïa.

Oh !

Well,   what's next ?.

" *Hello Kenneth.*
Thank you from the bottom of my heart for the trip to meet me. It's very nice of you to have done it. I appreciated the great honour you gave me.
Thank you for this wonderful gift you dropped off yesterday at my hotel. The scarf is beautiful, and the icing on the cake, it exhales your cologne. It's a delicate attention.
I came by this morning to tell you in person, but you were jogging.
So I'll leave you this message to tell you that I've decided to leave today.
Why ?
First of all because I need to return to my home as soon as possible. On the other hand, as there is no more me, there is no more you, there is no more "We", I find no reason to prolong unnecessarily my stay in this beautiful city which will remain forever etched

102   The day after in London

in my memory.
Even if, there was never have "We," I couldn't
help but love you with pure and sincere love.
My love for you is alive in my heart and I
will never forget you.
I couldn't tell you. I could not tell you how
much an embrace in your mighty arms would
have comforted me and carried me to heaven to
land the moon. I haven't been able to tell you
everything I'm writing to you. I was afraid
I'd scare you away. Forgive me if I have
wasted your time which is so precious.
Goodbye Kenneth.
Think of me from time to time.
I kiss you (as we usually say on Skype).
Maïa ".

Kenneth can't believe what he just read. Did
he read what he read? He is slightly dizzy. He
settles down at the foot of his bed and tries to
recover his spirits.

So he rushes to his smartphone and tries to
reach Maïa whose plane has just taken off.

Too late.

103   The day after in London

What else can he do but hope that, time will eventually erase her grief.

He read about ten times that letter that iced his blood.

He feels guilty for breaking her heart. How could he know what was smoldering in her, deep in her heart? How could he imagine that their words exchanged innocently by Skype interposed, could have caused so much hope and so much damage at the same time? How to fix that broken heart into a thousand pieces?

21

London, early afternoon. Maïa's plane is landing. She passes all the steps of control and can finally take a taxi.

During the route towards her house, she pulls out the blue silk scarf one last time and smells it for a long moment.

A curious idea crossed her mind: to open the taxi window and let it escape. The disappearance of this element that still connects her to Kenneth, may help her to mourn this "stillborn" love that continues to make her heart bleed.

But at the final moment when she was going to act, she gave up and puts the scarf back in the bottom of her bag.

The taxi arrives in front of his house. She pays, picks up her suitcase and goes home.

The house is empty. Henry is in the basement in his studio finalizing a project he's been working on for a few weeks.

Without unpacking her suitcase, Maïa went straight to bed in the position of the fetus. She's sobbing. She can't control herself. Her eyes are red from having crying and her rimmel around her eyes eventually faded, making her face pale.

In the late afternoon, going up in the house, Henry found her deeply asleep, still in this position of the fetus.

He doesn't understand and even worries about

seeing her dressed in bed, the suitcase next to the bed, the shoes scattered in the room.

He hesitates. He doesn't know what to do. Is she sick? Should he wake her up? He stands for a moment in front of the foot of the bed, watches her sleeping and then, leaves the room and moves into the living room.

He is split between anger and worry. The piece of paper that reminds him his wife's getaway, remained on the kitchen table in the same place.

A little later in the evening, Maïa emerged from her long and deep sleep. She got up quickly, undressed and walked to the bathroom to lounge in a hot bath.

Henry waits in the living room, waiting for her to enter the living room.

As in such circumstances, the offended spouse prepares a plea for his rights and stages his intervention at the appropriate time, showing a disapproving face and reprobative as possible, thus expressing his anger and disapproval. The conviction of the offending spouse is de facto acquired.

But by the time Maïa appeared in the living room, dragging herself to kiss him as she did every time she returned from her trips, Henry got up and walked out of the living room. Maïa then went to the kitchen to prepare the dinner.

The dinner took place in an almost monastic silence, under the furtive gaze of Henry, who until then had not sought or found the right opportunity to start the war against his wife.

Dinner quickly shipped, dishes washed, tidying up of the kitchen, then Maïa returned into the bedroom without having loosening her teeth throughout the evening.

She unpacks her suitcase, sorts her dirty laundry that she loads into the washing machine, launches her usual laundry program, goes to bed and falls asleep immediately. It must be said that the pills she had taken in Berlin the day before to try to sleep, had a delayed effect on her sleep cycle.

Henry spent a long moment in the living room, asking himself the causes of this sadness that darkened his wife's face. Two or three Brandy later, he decided to go to bed in turn.

The next day, when she woke up, she passed her head through the entrance of her husband's room to greet him.

Henry had already gone down to the studio, having fallen a little behind on the finalization of this project that has given him headache since the departure of his wife.

She goes down to greet him in the studio, then goes back to start her day.

Emptying the washing machine, cleaning the house from top to bottom, (this house left a little abandoned since her departure), inventory of the overdue mail.

And then, a look at her smartphone. Several attempts of appeal from Kenneth, but a single message in her message box, sent late in the evening :

" Honey, I'm in London. I came to get you. "

END .

The day after in London

Éditeur : BoD-Books on Demand, 12/14 rond point des
Champs   Élysées,   75008   Paris,   France
Impression: BoD-Books   on   Demand,   Norderstedt,
Allemagne
ISBN   :   9782322224616
Dépôt légal : May, 2020

The day after in London